Cosmo's
New Bike

...ones —
from David
xx
August 2020

David R Morgan

Illustrated by Anna Semenova

A2Z
PRESS

Cosmo's New Bike

Printed in the United States of America

A 2 Z Press LLC

PO Box 582

Deleon Springs, FL 32130

bestlittleonlinebookstore.com

sizemore3630@aol.com

440-241-3126

ISBN: 978-1-946908-55-1

Dedication

To Bex and Toby,
Who are my inspiration
and my magic!

Friday after school, Cosmo the Cavapoochon
was riding his old bike in the park.

Just then, Perdita the Persian and her cat gang rode their bikes close to Cosmo.

"Hey, doggy!" purred Perdita. "Watch this. I bet you can't do this on your old bike." Perdita rode her bike really fast and then she made her bike jump, twisting it cleverly in the air.

"Cool!" meowed Perdita's gang.
"Cool!" Cosmo marveled.
"Yes, indeed!" purred Perdita as she licked her paws.

"I'll bet I can do that," growled Cosmo softly. "Watch this," he said as he rode his old bike as fast as he could and twisted in the air.

The old bike came down with a crash!!! Cosmo came
down with a crash!!!!! "Oops!" groaned Cosmo.
Perdita and her cat gang laughed and laughed and laughed.

"Your bike is rubbish!" purred Perdita.
"Your bike is rubbish!" chorused the cat gang.
"Go away!" barked Cosmo.

Cosmo stared at his old bike. It looked
like a heap of scrap metal. The back
wheel was twisted. The front wheel was twisted too.

Cosmo pushed his wobbly old bike back home to Princess's
house. He propped it by the back door.
"I'll fix it in the morning," he said to himself.

The next morning, when Cosmo came out to
fix his bike, he found a bike propped
up by the back door...but it wasn't his bike.

This bike was silver and blue and it was brand new! "Wow!" exclaimed Cosmo. "A brand new bike!" He saw the name 'Info-Rider' on the side of the bike.

There was a small silver box on the front of the bike. "Hello," said a friendly voice coming out of the box. "Put on the helmet."

Cosmo obediently put on the helmet.
"Good, Cosmo. I'm all yours." said the voice.
"Wow!" exclaimed Cosmo.

Just then, Princess came to the back door.
"Thanks, Princess!" Cosmo barked gratefully.
"Thanks for what?" asked Princess.
"Thank you for my brand new bike," Cosmo replied.

Princess looked at Info-Rider. "I didn't get this for you!"
said Princess, "but it is obviously for you...so enjoy."
Cosmo jumped on the bike and rode away!

Suddenly, Info-Rider shouted, "LOOK OUT!"
"There's a tortoise racing his car around the corner."
Cosmo sped out of the way.
"Thanks, Info-Rider," Cosmo said.

"Your friends, Bex and Toby are in trouble," said Info-Rider.
"They're stuck in a shed."
"Where?" asked Cosmo.
"Near the old playground in the park," Info-Rider said.

Cosmo hurried to the park and found the shed by the empty playground. He heard howls for help.
"It's Bex and Toby!" cried Cosmo.
"Yes! We know it's us!" they cried back.
"Please get us out! The door is stuck fast!"

"There, by the side of the shed is a chain,"
said Info-Rider. "Attach it to the door
and to my frame."
Cosmo got off his bike and did just
as Info-Rider told him to.

"Now, ride!" said Info-Rider. "Power boost."
Cosmo pulled and pulled and with all the strength and speed
Cosmo could muster up, the chain pulled and the
door moaned and groaned. It creaked and squeaked.

Then, with a loud "CRACK!" the door came off its hinges.
Cosmo braked hard. He braked so hard that he left deep,
deep tire marks in the ground. "Just in time!" barked Bex and Toby.

"We're late for lunch."

Cosmo rode over the hill and came to a stream.
"I wish I could jump over this stream," he
whispered to himself.

"Then do," encouraged Info-Rider. "Let's jump!"
Cosmo jumped spectacularly over the stream!

"Look over there!" said Info-Rider.
"A bunch of pussy cats."
It was Perdita and her cat gang.

LOOK OVER THERE!

"Hey, doggy!" purred Perdita.
"What's that heap of scrap metal you're riding?"
"Cheek," said Info-Rider.
"This isn't scrap!" growled Cosmo. "This is Info-Rider."
"It's rubbish," hissed Perdita.
"It's rubbish," Perdita's cat gang chorused.

"I'll bet my bike can go faster!" challenged Perdita.
"Ok," said Cosmo. "Let's have a race."

Perdita rode really fast. Cosmo rode faster. Cosmo was in front of Perdita. Then...."LOOK OUT!" exclaimed Info-Rider. "DANGER AHEAD!"

Just as Perdita turned her wheel into Cosmo's bike,
Info-Rider shouted, "Let's jump!"
"Yes!" woofed Cosmo and
Info-Rider jumped high into the air.

Perdita shot right under Cosmo and Info-Rider
and landed in the stream with a huge SPLASH!
"WOW!" chorused the cat gang.
"COOL," said Cosmo and Info-Rider.
"OOPS!" spluttered Perdita.

Perdita was dejected as she sat in the stream.
She was wet. She was very wet.
She didn't like it one little bit.

"My bike is not rubbish," barked Cosmo
and he punched into the air.
Then he helped Perdita out of the stream.

And in the late afternoon, Cosmo
and Info-Rider rode happily home.

And Cosmo loved his new bike, Info-Rider, so much!

The End

David R Morgan lives in England. He is a talented full-time teacher and writer.

He has written music journalism, poetry and children's books. His books for children include : 'The Strange Case of William Whipper-Snapper', three 'Info Rider' books for Collins and 'Blooming Cats' which won the Acorn Award and was animated for television. He has also written a Horrible Histories biography : 'Spilling The Beans On Boudicca' and stories for Children's anthologies.

For the last 4 years he has been working on his Soundings Project with his son Toby, performing his own poetry/writing to Toby's original music. This work is on YouTube, Spotify and Soundcloud.

Other Books by David R. Morgan

And many more to come!

A2Z Press LLC

A2Z Press LLC
published this work.
A2Z Press LLC is a
publishing company
created by Terrie Sizemore
for the purpose
of publishing literary works by new
and aspiring writers. All content is
G-rated. We welcome your submissions
of ideas for children's literature as well
as adult and self-help topics.
Science and medicine, holidays and
other interesting topics are all welcome.
Submit queries to sizemore3630@aol.com or
PO Box 582
Deleon Springs, FL 32130

Visit our Website

Visit terriesizemorestoryteller.com or bestlittleonlinebookstore.com for our latest titles and gifts for everyone.

Other Books by
A 2 Z Press Authors

Eggnog the Bulldog

There is a Poem Inside of Me

How To Succeed In College

H is for Horse

The 23rd Psalm

D is for Dog

Golden Tales: Havoc in Rome

Chilly: The Lost Little Snowboy Ornament

Fairy Hairy Trouble

And More!

9 781946 908551